Recycling!

illustrated by Jess Stockham

Which box does this go in? What about this?

The recycling truck will pick these up.

Look at that! Where does it all come from?

What happens when the containers are full?

Do the clothes go here? What about shoes?

I'll empty these cans, then I'll help you.

Did you recycle the old batteries?

Don't use a bag unless you have to.

I'll put the peelings in the compost.

These cabbage leaves are for the rabbits.

These are too big. What else can I try on?

Look, a red jacket. I hope it fits me!

Nearly ready! Which seeds can I plant?

Carrots, beans, peas. Lots of vegetables!

The seeds will need lots of water to grow.

This will all turn into compost for the soil.

They're carrying our recycling to the truck.

It's all sorted into different compartments.

There's a roof garden! And solar panels!

You can borrow six books from the library.

I wonder who owned this toy.   Is it for sale?

That pot looks useful. How much is it?

Leave some strawberries for the jam!